CW00828758

Tom Investigates

Peter Chegwidden

The moral right of the author has been asserted.

No part of this publication may be reproduced, stored in a retrieval system or transmitted in any form or by any means without the prior permission in writing of the publisher, nor be otherwise circulated in any form of binding or cover other than that in which it is published and without a similar condition being imposed upon the subsequent purchaser.

This book is a work of fiction. Names, characters, businesses, organisations, places and events are either the product of the author's imagination or are used fictitiously. Any resemblance to actual persons, living or dead, events or locales is entirely coincidental.Copyright © 2016 Peter Chegwidden

All rights reserved.

ISBN: 1541146670

ISBN-13: 978-1541146679

INTRODUCTION

This is intended to be a simple, charming little fun story about cats.

These cats are not cartoon cats, or any sort of animated cats, they are just the neighbourhood cats we come across every day. Perhaps even your very own cat! They are cats behaving like cats just as we see them behaving every day.

But in this tale we allowed into their world. We hear them speak and learn what they are thinking.

It is a kiddies tale for adults. Just sit back, relax and enjoy!

Admittedly the adventures are very far-fetched but otherwise there would be no story. There are several interwoven threads and several very happy endings.

There is no bad language or anything to offend.

So come with us and get in touch with your feline side. We'll start by meeting Tom.

INTRODUCTION BY TOM

Hello. My name is Tom and I'm a cat. A tabby, so I'm told.

My kingdom is located in Minster on the Isle of Sheppey in Kent and my base is the home of my service providers, Sally and Martin.

They feed me delicious and nutritious food when I'm hungry, cuddle and caress me when I need affection, give me somewhere cosy to sleep indoors, empty and replenish my cat litter, and take care of my health needs. They also groom me and leave me looking like, well, the cat's whiskers!

And that enables me to lead my own life just as I please and for a cat that is a very satisfactory arrangement. I come and go as suits me and without a care in the world. My service provider, Martin, says I live the life of Riley, whatever that means. I've haven't ever come across a cat called Riley. Yet.

I have earned a well-deserved reputation for being a problem solver, and have unravelled a number of crimes and mysteries that have defeated lesser cats. The story you are about to read is one of those mysteries, and it was truly baffling I can tell you. In fact, it became quite a sinister and frightening affair.

Still, we cats are made of sterner stuff, and we do have our legendary nine lives to fall back on. Mind you, I have been in so many tight corners I could well be on overdraft there....

CONTENTS

Chapter One

Alfie sat quietly in the sun and watched the birds flit across the sky above his head.

Too high to catch. He'd learned that as a kitten. A waste of energy and, well, you look so foolish, leaping about waving your paws at thin air. His service providers, Kate and Hugh, used to laugh at his antics much to his annoyance.

Occasionally now he would remind them of those early years with a few moments of similar nonsense. It made them laugh. Crumbs, service providers are so easy to please, he'd reflect, and he would nearly always earn a treat, usually something tasty to nibble.

Alfie was proud of his appearance. Mainly white, with some black, some orange, some grey, he seemed to be the only cat of his kind in the neighborhood and it pleased him. Kate and Hugh groomed him to perfection and that only added to his vanity.

In fact, he couldn't understand why that chap over the road shouted at him when Alfie strolled through his garden. Really aggressive too. Alfie wondered if it was a case of mistaken identity when the man (or his wife) chased him, so much so that Alfie would pause and look back at his pursuer as if to say 'do you really mean me?' Sadly, the man always did.

He decided the couple had probably never been chosen as service providers for a cat so had little understanding. Perhaps he should pity them. If they had never been blessed to be chosen as service providers for a cat they had obviously missed out on one of life's wondrous joys. And he would forgive the man and his wife for their rants and pursuits. Poor devils, he reasoned.

Given his unusual colour scheme it probably never occurred to Alfie that he was ill-suited for under-cover work, yet he always yearned to join Tom on one of his adventures. That Tom, what a one for solving crime and all manner of mysteries! Alfie wished he was that clever. Still, at least he was Tom's closest friend, confidante and team-mate.

If Tom was Minster's Sherlock Holmes Alfie had to content himself by being Dr Watson.

A successful partnership if ever there was one, although, it had to be acknowledged, Tom often had to finish up rescuing Alfie from another close shave.

At that moment Alfie's mental meanderings were interrupted by Carla appearing on top of the fence. Carla, a tortoiseshell and proud of it, was Alfie's unattainable dream. Not in her class and he knew it. She had once told him that she didn't think Carla was her real name, and that when she was kitten she'd been shown an official looking piece of paper with the names Suzie-Anne Bluebelle on it. It had been explained to her that she was Suzie-Anne Bluebelle but that was the last she heard of it, and had been called Carla ever since.

Today she looked down almost sneeringly at Alfie and he instinctively looked away. You'll not tease me, my girl, he thought! In truth, time to move on, and he set off at a saunter, gave Carla a quick backward glance, and sprang up and over a wall and was on his way.

***

Angus hated his name. In fact, he refused to answer to it. He wasn't Scottish, nor a Scottish breed if there was such a thing, and he couldn't understand why his service providers had handicapped him with such a handle. They weren't Scottish either and they never went to Scotland in all his years on the planet. He'd assumed Angus had Scottish connections as visitors to Jill and Jason's home commented on the matter having asked what the cat's name was. What made the issue worse, and put Angus's back up, was that Jason often called him Gussie which Angus decided lacked the masculine strength of his proper name. Quite frankly, he thought it sounded rather feminine, and refused to answer to it even more than he routinely refused to answer to Angus.

Jill was a dream and he could wrap her round his paw. He had learned that a few me-ows in the right place accompanied by some leg rubbing and general nestling always produced food. Sitting in the kitchen looking at his empty dish usually came with the same result. And for that he was prepared to put up with some mild humiliation over his name.

Angus didn't like hot summer days as he possessed a thick, woollen coat which, he understood (well, he'd always been told), was to do with his breed. Nonetheless it was a boon on cold winter days! And there were summer days that were just like winter. Jill often grumbled about it.

"It's so cold it could be winter," she'd say.

7

Today was not one of those days. It was hot. And Angus preferred to be out and about nighttimes when the weather was like this. Having sought out Jill and been well fed he was now yawning and feeling happily sleepy. Pausing for a quick claw scratch on the old wicker chair, the one piece of furniture he was allowed to scratch, he curled up on an armchair (confident Jill wouldn't have the heart to move him) and settled down to a pleasant siesta.

Unaware that the night that was approaching was going to have serious consequences for him.

***

Tom was also yawning.

And stretching. And then having a cat's lick. He'd been dozing in the shade but as the sun had moved round so he had lost the shadow and was now awake and conscious of the fact he was peckish as well as warm.

He rose and ambled across the immaculately mown lawn, and with all the light-pawed agility of a young cat leapt up and over the gate and continued his stroll down the drive. This was one of his 'routes' and he knew it intimately.

'Hungry' replaced 'peckish' and he broke into a feline trot as he headed across the road. Two more gardens and he was on home territory. He was hoping the patio door would be open today for that was his preferred means of entry and exit. Much more comfortable than that wretched cat flap.

How he hated the thing. A narrow tunnel. Being claustrophobic he detested the device with a vengeance. He couldn't whistle and for that matter he couldn't hum, but on his way out through the cat flap the theme to '*The Great Escape*' would play in his mind.

In the other direction, going in, just past the cat flap was another vision of hell. The box Sally and Martin used to take him to the vet. It was little more than a small cage with precious little room to move. Humans don't treat each other like this when one takes another to the human's vet, he decided, so why am I demeaned like that?

It was like being a prisoner transported to court for judgment.

"Prisoner cat at the bar, you have been found guilty of being unwell. The sentence of this court is that we will stab you with a sharp needle. And may God have mercy on your soul."

8

Tom disliked injections as much as he hated the box and nearly as much as he loathed the vet.

Today the patio door was wide open and Tom was in like lightning, straight to the kitchen where Sally was standing by the sink peeling potatoes.

"Well, Tom, you old rascal, where *have* you been, eh? Where have *you* been?" she enquired in that lovely lilting voice she used to show affection, using much the same words she normally employed each time he put in an appearance. He was used to this and, being a cat, was not actually required to answer and to explain himself.

Whereas there had been that evening when he and Sally were home and Martin came in to face very similar questions. Tom had smiled inwardly and thought to himself that he bet Martin wished he was a cat, for there was no affection that time in Sally's voice, and she did actually want to know precisely where he'd been! *And* what he'd been doing!

Me, thought Tom, I'd've gone me-ow a few times, rubbed myself all around her legs and not had to tell her anything and been given a treat into the bargain! Humans, they could learn so much from us cats.

"Meee–owwww" whispered Tom recognising that Sally liked this soft approach best of all. Now for stage two. And he rubbed himself against her legs. And lo and behold his dish was filled with goodies and his dessert bowl was topped up with biscuits. A two course meal washed down with Adam's Ale, and all for the price of a me-ow and a leg rub.

He chuckled to himself. They can't get that up the pub by going me-ow and rubbing the landlord's leg.

After refreshments it was time to move out again. Perhaps Alfie would be in the 'usual' spot, in the shade under the back of Mr Simpson's car on the gentleman's drive. It was a good spot. A cat could rest peacefully there (Mr Simpson rarely went out by car), and observe all the comings and goings on that part of the road.

Yes, Alfie was there and Tom joined him. Tom listened. He pricked up his ears and turned his head slightly to better hear the approaching sound.

"It's Hartley," he observed before dropping his head back on to his front paws. It was widely acknowledged that Tom could detect another cat over a considerable distance and identify the creature from its paw-steps. Sure enough Hartley, a marmalade cat, hove into view and ambled over to join the pair of them.

Hartley was unique in that he had two nicknames.

He had never forgiven his service providers, Adam and Colleen, for calling him Hartley just because he was a marmalade, but he suspected the children may have had something to do with it. So he was often called Jam (by other cats) which he felt was somewhat mocking and perhaps even slightly rude. He preferred his other nickname Catnav.

Hartley probably knew every inch of Minster, having visited most gardens and all of its roads, could find his way around blindfold (so it was rumoured), and possessed a mental map of the area as a result of his wanderings. He knew Minster like the back of his paw.

He therefore knew all the ways of getting from A to B and exactly where to avoid unfriendly cats, aggressive dogs and unpleasant householders. Tom thought Hartley would've made an excellent taxi driver for he surely had 'the knowledge' as he thought it was called in London: the ability to instantly select the best and quickest route in any circumstances.

But Hartley rarely moved anywhere quickly. When exploring his district his two main speeds were dead slow and stop. Nonetheless, he could show a clean set of paws when the situation required alacrity and was probably the fastest, most agile cat on the island. Probably.

"Anything on for tonight, lads?" enquired Hartley whilst settling himself down with his friends under the car.

"Yep," replied Tom, "a dead of night performance for the benefit of that couple that shout at us and chase us when we wander across their garden.

"Good-O," enthused Hartley, "what's the form?"

"It's a three step plan, Hartley. First, we get beneath their bedroom windows and give them a recital of the cat's chorus. Then me and Alfie stage one of our famous catfights. Lots of noise, you know the form. Third, you hide behind a wall and make that noise like a human baby crying. You're very good at that, Hartley. And it always disturbs humans, does the trick every time."

"Love it, love it," Hartley chortled, and he followed up his mirth with a great deal of licking of his front paws, always a sign he was truly happy.

But the evening was not going to go entirely to plan, had they but known it.

***

Later Tom and Alfie were passing the time of day in some long grass somewhere.

"Nice chap, that Mr Simpson," commented Tom.

"Yep, don't think he's ever had a cat, though," added Alfie.

"I heard he's what is called a widower, whatever that is."

"Yes, that's right. He had a wife once, so she must've been a widow presumably."

"He could do with another widow I reckon."

"Yes, perhaps we could find him one, and then the pair of them could have a cat. I think they'd make excellent service providers."

"Couldn't agree more, Alfie, but no idea where we cats could find a spare widow."

"Even so, we can always keep our ears to the ground, you never know, Tom. You never know."

Chapter Two

Angus was roaming the streets.

It was chilly and just the way he liked summer. A chilly, dark night. Most of the street lights were out which enabled the cat to exercise what he freely admitted was a juvenile pleasure, activating the security lights on properties he passed.

There was one house where the sensor was particularly sensitive. He would move nearby and see the light come on, then withdraw and return as soon as it went off, so that it lit again. Great fun! His record was nine times on the trot, but at that stage the fun element had diminished and he slipped quietly away to pursue other interests.

One of these interests was a black cat called Milly. She had recently moved to the area from a far off distant land called Nottinghamshire and Angus had offered to show her around, having been smitten at their first meeting. He had been greatly touched by the way she called him Duck and had assumed it was her special nickname for him. He was in for a disappointment as it emerged she called all the cats, male and female, Duck.

Never mind.

Milly had accepted his invitation but had been very wary. She'd heard all about male cats from her mother who didn't have a good word for any of them, least of all her dad who had apparently deserted her mother before she and her siblings were born. Milly was about the age when a young cat develops an interest in the opposite sex, and she had found Angus particularly attractive but for reasons she couldn't quite place.

She'd never met anyone like Angus back home. He stood out in a crowd and had dark, smouldering looks that made her swoon.

So they often met at night and explored Minster together. Just being with her warmed the cockles of his heart. And he was always the perfect gentleman. Thus Milly gradually shed her wariness and caution and gave herself freely to swooning.

What brought them closer together was the night Milly was wandering alone when she turned into an alley there to be confronted by one very large, angry male cat. Hissing and spitting he showed his claws and his flaming enraged eyes bore deep into her own and she was afraid. Very.

From nowhere (so it seemed) Angus flew past her and put the scoundrel to flight.

That was the night Angus and Milly shared their first cuddle. And very beautiful it was too. And Milly swooned like she had never swooned before. And Angus was engulfed in exquisitely delightful warm feelings he had never known before. They purred contentedly together as the starlit sky watched over them and bestowed paradise upon them.

Tonight Angus was abroad on his own and following one of his well trodden routes. Whether he was dreaming of Milly or his mind had wandered to other matters he was unable to recall later.

His sixth sense had deserted him and he had no indication that danger was close.

He was just passing Mr Simpson's place, was only slightly aware of Tom and his mates making a hullabaloo up the road, when disaster struck.

What seemed to Angus like an enormous fox had him by the throat. This huge creature, growling and dribbling, had taken the cat completely by surprise and he wanted his dinner. Angus wanted his life. Angus couldn't even cry out in despair or pain but he knew, just knew, he was fighting for survival. And he fought.

Momentarily he thought about Tom up the road but there was no way of alerting him. In this life and death struggle neither cat nor fox heard footsteps, human footsteps, but all of a sudden there was a clatter and a great deal of objectionable human language as a dark figure fell over the fighting animals.

The fox deserted the scene. A relieved but terrified Angus looked at the prone figure in the road who was gingerly picking himself up, still cursing, and checking the bag he had with him. Tom, Alfie and Hartley, having heard the kerfuffle, arrived and were pleased to see their friend in one piece, though badly shaken, but were curious about the man and what he might be doing in the middle of the night.

The man was away.

Then a light came on in Mr Simpson's bungalow, then another. The front door opened and a pyjama-clad Mr Simpson stood in the doorway waving his walking stick.

"Come back here, you ... you ... devil you! Come back here. I'm calling the police, damn you. Come back here, come back...." But his voice trailed away as he started to cough and splutter.

Tom was the first to realise what had happened. An intruder had broken into Mr Simpson's, had probably stolen some valuables, and made good his escape. Quick as thought he sent Hartley off in pursuit of the burglar, Hartley being the fastest cat present. Poor, poor, dear Mr Simpson, he thought, he didn't deserve that.

What a shame the intruder's collision with Angus and the fox hadn't disabled him in some way! Tom realised immediately that, distressed though he was, Angus was the only one to have seen the burglar's face, so perhaps he could get a description. If he's escaped on foot good old Hartley will follow him to the ends of the earth, which, as far as Tom knew, lay just beyond Sheerness.

Mr Simpson's front door was now shut but one or two other house lights had come on nearby, probably as a result of the commotion and the shouting.

"Funny, isn't it?" Angus said, "In a strange way I owe that intruder my life! Poor Mr Simpson. Wonder what's been taken?"

Tom was busy thinking, and did even more thinking before answering.

"Well, I expect the police will be here soon. I wonder how Catnav's doing?"

***

Tom was suffering from curiosity. All very natural, of course, he being a cat.

He was curious about why the police never came. Hartley had been quite brilliant on what proved to be a fruitless chase. It is doubtful any other cat on the island could so comprehensively have covered so much ground, so many roads and alleys, and done so with such strategic purpose.

He had criss-crossed an ever-enlarging grid and done so at incredible speed, but of the thief there was no sign. This led Tom to believe the intruder either had a car handy (though none was heard at the time) or lived close by.

Angus was not much use as a witness. Fair enough, he had been terrified and had been wrestling for his life, fighting for breath, just before he caught sight of the burglar's face. And it *was* pitch dark, after all. Nevertheless, his descriptions varied widely each time he recounted them.

"Perhaps the fox fancied a catburger," Alfie had said, rudely, and made matters worse, and his offence the greater, by adding, "Or given your appearance, Angus, maybe that should be a woollyburger!" Happily Angus saw the funny side. Eventually.

None of this helped Tom. He was already beginning to wonder if what they had witnessed had been a completely different scenario altogether.

Unlikely.

But no police. Strange that. Unless, of course, Mr Simpson disturbed him and frightened him off before he could steal anything. But you'd still ring the police, surely?

Hartley had worn himself out but Tom had to admit he'd done a smashing job and left no stone unturned. No way could the intruder have eluded him.

Tom being, in his own terminology, '*head cook and bottlewasher*' for the Minster Cats Neighbourhood Watch, he swiftly put the word out about the fox and about the supposed burglar, although sadly he had no good description of the latter to add to it.

Local foxes had always appeared to be relatively small, scrawny creatures, a serious threat for kittens maybe, but not usually for wide-awake adult cats. Was there a monster on the loose?

Problems. Problems.

"Alfie?"

"Yes, Tom."

"What happens when we nestle up to a human, especially a cat lover?"

"Well, I get my throat tickled and my tummy rubbed."

"Anything else?"

"Mmmmm ...... well, my service providers tend to talk to me, like the way they talk to human babies. You know, goo-goo-goo-who's a lovely puss-puss then, all that kind of thing."

But an idea had formed in Tom's fertile mind.

"Alfie, Mr Simpson always seems a nice gentleman, doesn't he? I mean, he's not had a cat in my lifetime, but he doesn't shout at us and doesn't do anything when we walk across his garden. I wonder..."

"What do you wonder, Tom? What do you wonder?" Alfie was used to Tom coming up with ideas and was inclined to take all this thinking with a pinch of salt.

"I thought I'd go over to Mr Simpson's, when he's in his garden, nestle up and see if he'll talk to me, perhaps tell me something interesting. You know, sometimes humans confide in their cats if there's something on their minds."

"Okay Tom, let me know how you get on..." and Alfie rolled onto his side, stretched, yawned, licked his front paws and curled into a ball ready for sleep. Tom decided his dear friend could not have been less interested in his plan and possibly, for that matter, in Mr Simpson's plight.

***

Peering over the fence and clinging on by his claws Tom observed Mr Simpson sitting in the garden reading the paper. He was in that old picnic chair that looked most unsafe and was wearing a boater as he so often did in the summer. An open-necked shirt and a pair of light trousers, together with open-toed sandals, completed the picture. A man at peace.

Well, maybe not so. I wonder, thought Tom, if he misses his widow?

In an instant he was over the fence and trying to appear as nonchalant as possible ambled in a meandering, roundabout way towards the figure on the patio. Mr Simpson saw him at the last moment and Tom froze. They stared at each other. Mr Simpson moved first, resting the paper in his lap and decorating his face with a beautiful smile. Tom unfroze and took a step nearer.

"Hello puss, hello puss," Mr Simpson began, "You're a lovely puss-puss, aren't you. My, what a lovely puss you are. Now, have you come to see me? Would you like me to stroke you? There's a good puss, there's a good puss."

Dear me, thought Tom, just like Alfie said. Goo-goo-goo.

So he took a gamble and leapt into Mr Simpson's lap, crushing the copy of the Telegraph in the process.

But Mr Simpson was indeed a very kindly old man and took to the visit with immense pleasure, laughing, cuddling and stroking Tom, and generally making a fuss of him. Tom put up with all this. He was a cat on a mission, and besides he found he was enjoying all the attention.

The kindly old man chatted away for a while in much the same inane style previously employed, but then he sat back and the smile slipped away.

"I don't know your name, puss, but I'm Albert Simpson and I'm pleased to make your acquaintance. I'm pleased to see you even if you're not staying long. I expect you'll dash back home soon and forget all about me. And I will be left alone with my sadness.

"I don't suppose you know or care that I'm sad, dear puss, but I am. I awoke last night and thought I heard a noise. And, do you know, when I investigated, I had a burglar. Yes I did. He took flight as soon as he saw me, but I collected up my walking stick and chased him out the door just to be on the safe side. Oh, if you could've seen me, dear puss, in my jim-jams, chasing after a man probably half my age!

"I rang the police and they gave me a crime number. For my insurance purposes. At that stage I didn't know anything had been taken. Luckily he'd only got as far as going through my bureau. But here's the sad bit, dear puss. He'd taken a solid gold locket that belonged to my late wife, Emily. It contained a photo of each of us on our wedding day. Emily always wore it, until her dying day, dear puss."

"Still, as if you care dear puss!" And Tom saw the tears in his eyes as Mr Simpson looked up the garden, his memories swamping his heart and his mind. Tom sat up and started licking the man's face and the smile and the laughter returned which quite made Tom's day.

Because the news he'd just heard had otherwise shattered it.

Chapter Three

Another day. Another summer's day. Hot. Wall-to-wall sunshine and blue skies.

Alfie had tired of annoying the McCaskell's terrier and left the dog hot, exhausted, angry and distressed. And probably with a sore throat too. All that barking. Alfie knew just how long the lead was and had learned (admittedly the hard way) to check first that it was attached to the dog's collar.

He gave the terrier one of his best smiles as he tormented him over a distance of roughly eighteen inches. Had it been physically possible for a cat he would've blown him a kiss for good measure.

But there is only so much pleasure one can get in such circumstances and, in any case, Alfie realised it was most likely time to go and find Tom.

Alfie couldn't believe how cruel someone had been to that lovely Mr Simpson and he felt strongly that they ought to do all they could to find him a widow to replace the one he'd lost. Of course, he knew there could be no replacement as such for his beloved Emily, but he thought that a new widow would be good company and might actually encourage them to adopt a cat.

He further considered that a new widow might have a cat of her own to bring into the relationship.

Tom's patio door was closed and Alfie could see Tom stretched out inside occupying almost the whole cover his service providers placed on the sofa for Tom's use. No good trying the cat flap. Alfie had been invited in once but the flap wouldn't open except for Tom. Something to do with his 'chip' whatever that is. This was truly a technologically advanced cat flap, obviously designed to keep all other cats out.

But, as they had discovered, it kept invited friends out too.

Alfie's was a simple device and he often invited friends in. Kate and Hugh and their daughters welcomed Tom but Kate and Hugh didn't seem so keen when Alfie invited half the cats in the neighbourhood in. Strange creatures, humans.

Sally saw Alfie sitting outside quietly me-owing and slid open the patio door. Alfie was as welcome at Tom's as Tom was at Alfie's.

"Look who's here to see you, Tom, look who's here, just look who's here," Sally advised in her sweet but rather patronising voice. Tom glanced across at the visitor, stretched, shifted slightly and closed his eyes again. Alfie would understand. Alfie did. In fact Alfie simply sprang up and joined his mate on the sofa and the two snuggled down together.

Friendship.

However, Tom conceded barely an inch of sofa, hardly moving, so Alfie had to make do best he could but, being a cat, managed it without quite looking comfortable. But comfortable he was, in a way only cats can be when seemingly screwed up in a misshapen ball. It was an altogether an agreeable start to their meeting!

***

Later they strolled peacefully in the sunshine. Tom decided Alfie had got humans sussed. Yes, they do tend to treat us like human babies, goo-goo-goo and all that. But we get well looked after in the main. Alfie interrupted his train of thought.

"Tom, what can we do about poor Mr Simpson?"

"I think every possible task is darn nigh impossible. Find his intruder, find the locket, find him a replacement widow. Dear me, it's a bother, Alfie, it's a bother.

Alfie considered the problems for a while, resolved that they were all beyond his powers of reasoning and allowed his mind to slip back into neutral where it was comfortable and at ease. Tom, however, was weighing up all the issues and trying to find solutions, and came to a conclusion.

"What you have to do, Alfie, is look at the balance of probabilities. We may never find the intruder and the locket is possibly miles away now, or at the very least is going to be sold on the black market. And we don't actually know exactly what it looks like. Now, as far as finding a spare widow is concerned, well, we cats have access to most people's properties, right? So how about we organise a scout round, see if we can locate a lonely widow who might want a cat and a widower. In that order, of course."

Alfie nodded agreement but their discourse came to a premature end as Angus came bolting towards them. Puffing and blowing (he was very hot in his thick coat) he gasped out his news.

"Quick lads, the Broadway, just seen the intruder coming out of Londis and heading for a blue Fiesta parked in Noreen Avenue. As soon as I saw his face I knew, really *knew* it was him."

Angus had re-arranged Tom's priorities in one fell swoop, and the three of them bounded down Queenborough Drive, across the Broadway and into Noreen. No blue Fiesta.

"Did you get the registration?" Tom asked rather urgently.

"Er ... I ... er ... no ...er ...sorry Tom," a crestfallen Angus replied.

"He can't have gone far. I'll nip down Noreen, Alfie nip round into Minster Road, Angus you'd better get your breath back. Stay here in case he returns another way."

And with that Angus went to look for some shade in the doctor's surgery car park while Tom whizzed along Noreen Avenue at a pace that would've done Hartley justice. Alfie paused briefly at the junction with Minster Road, as the road went up as well as down, elected to go westwards and set off at speed.

None of the cats experienced success.

The car had vanished as the intruder had done the other night. The three met up again and it was Angus who spoke.

"I didn't get the reg, sorry guys, but I remember now that it had a big dent and a bit of red paint on the offside rear wing, Must've been in a bash at some time." Tom was well pleased. Every bit as good as the registration number!

"Okay, we know he lives round here, and we've a telling description of his car, so that's narrowed the field. Let's go and find Catnav and see if we can come up with a plan for searching the whole area in a totally efficient manner tonight. It's too hot now, and anyway, if he hasn't gone straight home his car won't be there. We need all the paws we can get. So lads, spread the word, and we'll meet on the open land between Fleetwood Close and Blatcher Close at 9 p.m. this evening."

***

The job was right up Hartley's street. It required military precision and military execution and Hartley was the only cat who could've masterminded such an operation. His planning was superb. But then he knew Minster intimately and knew precisely how to use his resources (the other cats) to maximum benefit.

Every road and parking spot was covered. There was always an outside chance the car would be in a garage but Tom thought that most unlikely.

Hartley was using an extensive search area and incorporating Halfway to the west, Thistle Hill to the south, and Minster all the way eastwards to Kingsborough Manor. It was an enormous area but given enough cats Hartley's strategic planning would do the trick with nobody duplicating anyone else.

There was quite a buzz on the open land that night and for once it wasn't the bees. Hartley counted up and found he had twenty three cats at his disposal, twenty four including himself.

His grid search plan included an intricate communications network so that if the car was located the search could be swiftly concluded without further ado, and the searchers released from their duties.

Having assigned the cats to their routes Hartley had one last thing to say.

"One more point. Don't get carried away. Remember that Angus here was attacked by a monster fox the other night. Keep your eyes open and your wits about you. Stay safe." All the cats nodded having been reminded that they travelled this night, as all others, at their own peril.

And so they spread out and set off as darkness fell.

It was Carla who found it. By dead reckoning the search had thus far taken only about a quarter of an hour and Carla was beside herself with excitement. There on the Harps estate by the roadside, the damage to the rear offside as clear as day. She sent up the special call sign me-ow to alert her local controller, who happened to be Angus, and Angus despatched his team to the other sectors to call off the operation.

Hartley was like a cat with two tails. Pride was his middle name. In fact, his smug grin was lighting up the dark sky!

The chorus seemed to be 'Well done Catnav' and 'Only Catnav could've done that'. And they were right. First, as they re-assembled on the open land, there was a roll call to make sure everyone was back, and then Hartley thanked everyone and said he was bursting with pride at the enthusiasm and skill with which all had taken part. Tom thanked Carla and, as the meeting broke up with every cat in fine mood, and talking about the adventure, he, Carla, Alfie and Hartley made their way to the parked car.

But which house?

Only one thing for it. Alfie volunteered to sit tight till morning and Tom would take the next shift until such time as the man went to his car. If necessary they would run a rota guard system all day and all next night if nobody appeared.

"You were really clever and observant, Carla," said Alfie, hoping to gain some brownie points with his dream cat. None was available, or at least none was offered.

"Did my job, Alfie, don't make such a big thing of it," she responded before cocking her nose in the air and sauntering off towards the west end of Harps Avenue. Alfie felt deflated and snuggled down on the grass verge, keeping watch.

Tom stayed a while, for company, prior to heading home.

It was quite dark, warm and very quiet. After an hour or so Alfie became bored and inevitably was overtaken by sleep.

He woke to the sound of a sudden crack. Still dark, still warm, still quiet. Apart from the crack, that is. In that instant he was gripped by fear and started shaking and trembling. All at once memories of the terrible attack on Angus flooded his mind.

So without further consideration he shot up the nearest tree. It was just as well that he did for what he saw next turned his stomach and frightened the life out of him.

He'd never seen such a big fox. It had to be Angus's. And it was on the prowl for food. Thank heavens, Alfie thought, that Carla's long gone. The fox showed no signs of moving on and even came and had a sniff at Alfie's tree.

It was crystal clear to Alfie that the fox smelled cat, which was hardly surprising bearing in mind how long Alfie had been lying in the grass beneath. The fox also appeared to have made up his mind that the cat was up the tree. Further, the fox obviously felt sure the cat would come down some time soon, perhaps in time for breakfast, for he hung about and slowly and menacingly circled the tree. He kept looking up as if he could see rather than just sense his quarry.

Perhaps he could.

And poor Alfie shook and felt very, very alone.

***

Sunrise.

Tom stretched. Thought about it then yawned, yawned a cavernous yawn, thought some more, stretched and yawned at the same time and started licking his paws. Then he licked his tum. Satisfied with the results of his cat lick he stretched and yawned some more.

Then he remembered the night. And next he remembered Alfie standing guard over the blue car. It all came back to him. His next piece of memory recall advised him that he was due to take over from his friend, and in all probability right now.

One stretch, that should do it, and Tom eased off the sofa and stared at the cat flap. Darn thing. How he hated it. Still, needs must, and he flew at the device, heard the click, and he was past the flap and into and out of the tunnel. Sigh of relief.

It was still very early. Perhaps it was too early to relieve Alfie. Tom looked back at the cat flap, decided he'd had enough of that for now and resolved to go on.

Thus is was that he set out for Harps. Slowly. Gently does it, no need to rush. And his stroll was accompanied by various extensive yawns. Looking up he saw a pigeon looking down warily. The pigeon was on a branch and for all appearances seemed to be making sure Tom passed by without disturbing him.

Plenty of birdsong. Tom liked birdsong. Well, he liked birds. That is, he didn't mind chasing them since that was what cats were supposed to do, but he had no real desire to catch one. He'd brought one home once as a thank you for Sally and Martin, but it hadn't been appreciated as the gift it was intended to be. Sally had something Martin called hysterics and Martin chased Tom and the bird out of the house.

Happily, although undoubtedly distressed and afraid, the bird flew away none the worse for the encounter and flew away uninjured. Since then Tom hadn't bothered. Oh well, if that's all the thanks you get for coming home with a treasured gift.....

He crossed the Minster Road. No traffic this time of day. Then he walked his slow, measured walk along the alley beside the library and headed up to where Alfie would be waiting.

But what he saw next stopped him in his tracks.

***

Hartley was curled up on the bed twixt Adam and Colleen. He had free run of the house at all times and was permitted on the marital bed. He had snuggled down, a very contented puss. He was feeling very self-satisfied and proud, as indeed he might, for his organisational skills coupled with his intimate knowledge of Minster had brought about a swift and satisfactory conclusion to the evening's business.

Well done Catnav indeed. Now he was tired. He drifted off to sleep thinking about what the next steps in this unusual adventure would be and it was then that he recalled the fox. He found he had startled himself awake, but dismissing the cause of his aggravation he soon closed his eyes and slept again.

But he did not sleep peacefully.

He suffered a dreadful nightmare. An enormous fox, with long, sharp fangs, horns like a bull and making a roaring noise that would've woken the dead, had hold of poor Alfie and was shaking him like a rag doll. If he had been human Hartley would've woken and screamed but he did the cat equivalent, trembling and squealing and waking his service providers into the bargain.

He threw himself off the bed and dashed down the stairs, into the kitchen and out the cat flap and stood breathing deeply and hurriedly as he regained his senses. Then he recalled where Alfie was and that Alfie was all alone.

Had he had a premonition perchance?

Only one thing to do and he set off a-pace hoping it wasn't too late, always assuming his nightmare had been some sort of omen.

Intermission

Tom writes:

"As you will have gathered this was quite an adventure, and I've had a few. Well, what cat hasn't?

Most adventures I have become embroiled in have had an element of risk but this one had real danger.

"I haven't before had the opportunity to describe one of my escapades as I cannot use a computer or an i-pad or an i-paw of whatever they're called. I don't even have a mobile phone – I wouldn't know where to start! Happily I have been able to dictate my story to my good friend Peter who has patiently typed the words and cheerfully put up with me when I want to change something, or want my neck rubbed, or want some grub or whatever.

"I get on very well with my cat friends Alfie (in particular) and Hartley and we usually spend some time together every day. So you will understand when I say that I knew writing the end of Chapter Three would be hard for the memories are still painful and so very sad. I shudder even today when I recall the events of that fateful night. Poor Alfie.

"When you have friends you know really well you feel a very special kind of affection for them; you share their joy when things are good and you share their sorrow and pain when it's all gone wrong. Friends can be as close as brothers and sisters. I have to confess that I've lost contact with my three sisters and one brother as they were given up for adoption as kittens, I suppose just as I was.

"What a shame there wasn't a service provider who wanted five kittens. Now I ask you, what cat lover wouldn't adore five mischievous kittens? Then we could've stayed together forever.

"So you will appreciate that Alfie and Hartley are like brothers to me and the thought of losing one of them would be indescribably painful.

"If the end of Chapter Three was difficult to write then you can well imagine Chapter Four was agony. But to Chapter Four we must all go together."

Chapter Four

Tom was suddenly aware of company. Hartley had drawn alongside and instantly seen the problem, the hideous problem.

Alfie up the tree shaking (appropriately) like a leaf, the fox seated at the base waiting for his breakfast to descend. And what a size that fox was; they'd never seen anything like it.

The fox was hoping for a cat takeaway, Alfie was hoping for a cat getaway.

"Leave this to me," said Hartley and, appearing much braver than he actually felt, he set off at a stroll across the road. The fox looked up and then sat up and finally rose to its paws. Hartley knew his own life depended on how quick his reactions were and, whilst he had no doubts about his reactions and his ability to sprint, realised that an error of judgment by a second or a few inches could mean his downfall.

As Hartley ambled up to the fox Tom took a mighty intake of breath. For pities sake Hartley, he thought, don't go any closer, please don't. But Hartley did. By now the fox had lost interest in the cat in the tree and had decided he fancied some marmalade for breakfast. And breakfast was three feet away.

He pounced like lightning but landed on empty ground. Hartley had sprung out of the way and missed death by a split second. Now the chase was on. The fox pursued Hartley but the wily cat swiftly worked out the fox's maximum speed and adjusted his own in order to keep clear, just, and to ensure the fox continued to hunt him down. This selfless and courageous action gave Alfie time to escape.

When Hartley was confident that he had put sufficient distance between the fox and Alfie, in fact he had done so by three or four streets, he accelerated and pulled well clear of the beast. In seconds he had vanished from view and the fox came to a halt, exhausted, frustrated, and in the meantime Alfie and Tom had run off the other way.

Eventually all three cats met near the top of Glenwood Drive and Alfie was all over Hartley like a rash.

"You saved my life, you brave, brave cat," he whimpered and Hartley was completely overwhelmed, literally, for Alfie was making a very physical fuss of his saviour as well as praising him verbally non-stop.

Of course, they didn't get to see where the car driver (the intruder) lived, but that was now a minor consideration.

News spread like wildfire and the modest, self-effacing Hartley was the toast of the town and every cat wanted to shake his paw. For himself he wasn't at all happy with all the hero worship and glory, but it had the very agreeable outcome that all the cats now called him Hartley or Catnav, his disliked nickname Jam consigned to history forever.

There was another agreeable outcome. A pretty and attractive young cat called Cha-cha (herself a marmalade) was making eyes at him and bestowing large amounts of hero worship upon him. Hartley was surprisingly shy and coy and really didn't know how to respond any more than he understood the lovely warm feelings he was getting inside for the first time.

The two became firm friends but it was clear Cha-cha wanted a very close friendship. Very. And it was becoming increasingly obvious to Hartley that he might just welcome it.

***

Back to the day job.

Tom still needed to know where the intruder lived in case there should be any chance of searching the premises and finding the locket.

He called on Angus who suggested keeping watch ought to be a two cat affair, for safety reasons and for as long as the fox was at large. He'd had his own brush with the animal. Alfie had been reluctant to take a turn of duty as well he might be and Tom wasn't sure whether he could ask Hartley after all that wonderful cat had been through.

He needn't have worried. Hartley willingly volunteered, if only as a means of temporarily escaping the attentions of Cha-cha, and Angus was more than willing to work with the hero of the hour.

So that night Hartley and Angus took the overnight shift with Tom and a black cat called Bubbles ready to take over at dawn. Tom wasn't keen on involving girls but Bubbles told him it was all about equality these days, and she wanted to be on the front line, she being every bit as good as he was. Bubbles stood her ground and Tom gave in. Fortunately, from his point of view, she showed no interest in him as a male cat so no danger there!

As the first signs of daybreak skirted the eastern horizon Tom made his way towards Harps and joined Bubbles at the pre-arranged rendezvous. Together, and with great alertness, they made their way across to the car. Hartley was up the tree as lookout and Angus was prowling around below. Angus had forgotten himself once and dashed off in pursuit of a mouse, only to be summoned back by Hartley, and duly reprimanded.

Bubbles elected to go up the tree and Tom patrolled the area around the car. Eventually the early morning sun put in an appearance and a certain warmth began to engulf their surroundings. People stirred from their slumbers and gradually human beings came upon the scene. However, it was clear their quarry was either not an early riser or had no reason to go out by car. Bubbles suggested a role swap and Tom nipped up the bark and made observations all around him.

No fox.

Well, it was more unlikely now it was daytime.

No intruder.

Was their wait going to be in vain? Tom hadn't bothered to arrange a following shift since he had assumed that by late morning it would be unnecessary. As time went by he was dreading Bubbles asking him who was taking over and then getting an earful when he told her there was nobody.

He was quietly fearful of being told he was a 'typical male'.

At the eleventh hour his blushes were saved before he could become a victim of female retribution. An ugly looking man, tall and thin, dressed in a dirty t-shirt, ragged jeans and rough looking suede shoes, came out of a door, coughed and choked and spluttered and made his way to the car. Success! They had the address. Once in the driver's seat he wound down the window and spent the next few moments rolling a cigarette, a horrible looking creation, all out of shape and with bits of tobacco sticking out at random from each end. He placed it between his lips and coughed at length as if anticipating its effects. The match set fire to the opposite end and a cloud of smoke was sucked out of the car via the open window.

He pulled on his seat belt, started the car and drove off. Tom was now at Bubbles's side.

"What you gonna do now?" she asked in a manner suggesting she presumed he hadn't thought that through. But he had.

"I'm going to slip round the back, see if I can see anyone else indoors, and if there's a window open I might be able to get in and have a look round," he replied.

"Mmmm ... well, just be careful. I'll keep watch. He might come back very soon, but I'll find a way of letting you know. Don't be long, I'd like to be sure you're safe." Tom was quite touched by this show of concern, but the look on Bubbles's face led him to believe it was more a case of impatience and an unwillingness to intervene in any 'trouble'.

So he set off. From the back garden he could see no other person, but wait, what was that? Aha, a cat flap in the kitchen door. Tentatively he crawled on all fours looking for all the world like a lion creeping up on its dinner. He tried the flap and it opened. He climbed inside. Not a pretty sight, in fact a rather dirty unkempt kitchen, and a smell of stale something or other, he couldn't make out what. An empty cat's dish and bowl of water stood in a corner.

He started.

"That you, my darling little Figaro, has my little baby-waby come home for his din-dins?" The female voice was reaching down from upstairs and sounded more like a strangled screech than, for example, Sally's pleasant tones. Figaro? *Figaro?* Sad name for a cat, Tom concluded. And din-dins. Yes, Alfie was right, they treat us like human babies. Din-dins indeed! And he was out of the door in a flash there now being no chance of a hunt round inside.

He returned to Bubbles to explain and it was she who spotted it.

"Wait a mo, Tom, I don't know of a cat called Figaro, do you?"

"No, Bubbles, that's true, very true. You're right, you know, we must have a stranger in our parish."

"Well done, Inspector Rebus," she added sarcastically. "And may I suggest a visit to old grumpy."

"Bubbles, don't be disrespectful to your elders. Patches may be a an old cat now but he deserves some respect in his autumn years. He may be slow but he's very knowledgeable and wise. And he's only grumpy cos all his joints creak and he can't dash about like he used to."

"Thanks for the lecture, Tom. Point taken anyway, Can I come with you?"

"Of course you can, Bubbles, let's go now."

With that they slipped away to find the wisest cat in Minster. Patches was basically white but had a few small black spots, hence his name, and he was not only a very wise cat he was almost certainly the oldest in town, if not the universe. If anyone knew of a Figaro he would, or if he didn't he would know how best to find out about him.

***

Alfie was recovering from his ordeal and applying his mind to another aspect of their supposed tasks, finding a replacement widow for Mr Simpson. He jumped up as a van drove past. He was sure it said '*replacement widows and doors*' on the side, so he gave chase. But when the van stopped he saw it actually read *windows* and not *widows*, and he felt very foolish.

"You're a lovely, beautiful pussy, aren't you? Oh, what a beautiful cat you are. Where *did* you get all those wonderful colours from? Come here, puss, would you like a cuddle-wuddle from auntie Joyce?"

Alfie stood stock still and turned his head to see where the voice was coming from. A delightful old lady, grinning from ear to ear, was edging ever closer and rubbing her fingers together as if she was offering Alfie a treat from her hand. She made some indescribable noises with her lips which Alfie mistakenly took for birdsong impressions.

"Auntie Joyce give beautiful cat beautiful cuddle, yes, would you like that my little sweetie-pie."

He listened to her words and didn't move a muscle. He had to admit she looked very cuddly, very cuddly indeed, being pleasantly rotund, and she certainly had a kind face which added an aura of happiness and warm-heartedness to her appearance. But after his encounter with the fox he was too wary and, as she advanced, he turned tail and raced away.

It was on his way back home that he chanced upon Tom and Bubbles and heard their tale. Needless to say he wanted to join them and the three went looking for Patches.

***

They found Patches resting in some long grass behind the Abbey Hotel, one of his favoured spots.

Sadly, he was indeed grumpy as usual, a state that he blamed on a bad back and a poor day's sleep, he being a night cat as a rule.

But he listened patiently to all they had to say about everything and closed his eyes to concentrate his thoughts. Bubbles assumed that he'd dropped off and gave him a playful nudge which was far from appreciated, a fact he grumpily acquainted her with.

Tom thought that he reminded him of Sally when she was doing something odd called (so he believed) yoga. Patches remained still, his eyes closed. The three cats looked at each other and occasionally glanced at Patches. At long last (an eternity it seemed to the trio) the old cat opened his eyes, looked at each of them in turn in a very deliberate way, and then spoke.

This is what he said:

"I have heard about the fox. He has no mate or family to feed. He eats for his own pleasure and devours farmers' chickens as well as any small creature he can lay his paws on. He is not a child of our island, he comes from a land far away from where he was banished for his uncaring ruthlessness and greed.

"It is said he crossed the great bridge realising it was unguarded. It is possible the humans will catch him, for we certainly cannot. For the moment be vigilant my children. Harm will come to him, so be patient. In time the threat will pass.

"Figaro I know of although I have not met him. He keeps his own company and, to the best of my knowledge, does not mix with any other cats. He keeps clear. He shuns contact. This may not be his fault, it may be that something unpleasant happened in his kittenhood and the memory stays with him to the present day and affects his life accordingly. I know precious little of his background so do not know how or where he came to be adopted. Please bear this in mind: he may be a rescue cat, someone a kind service provider has given a home to after ill-treatment elsewhere. Be tolerant and try to be understanding if you ever meet him.

"I understand he is a tabby, like you Tom, if that helps.

"There is nothing to suggest he is in any way evil like the intruder. But he may be aggressive if he catches you in his home. Nonetheless that is sadly the best chance you have of finding the locket if it is still there, of course. So proceed with caution, proceed with caution.

"I can see no way of letting Mr Simpson know the address of his intruder but I will think on. I will also give thought as to any possible way we can persuade the intruder to repent, give up his life of crime, and hand back the locket, if he still has it.

"But I fear the worst, my loves. I earnestly believe we may be able to do nothing about these issues. I will let you have word if I think of anything, but in the meantime do please let me know how things progress.

"Watch out for that fox. And go carefully, my precious ones. Now leave an old cat in the peace he deserves!"

Which is what they did.

Chapter Five

Alfie was ambling back with Tom when he happened to mention his encounter with 'Auntie Joyce'.

"Don't suppose she's a replacement widow," Tom commented without conviction. Alfie thought about this and his face lit up. Why, that might be the very case!

"Shall we go and try and find out?" he asked, all enthusiasm and energy, but Tom just gave him a sideways look that left him feeling slightly deflated. So Alfie decided to go anyway and bade his friend goodbye.

He soon located Auntie Joyce's house but it looked all locked up and the car was gone from the drive. Now he felt truly deflated. And his feelings were not improved when Carla walked by and totally ignored his greeting. Alfie turned his head and watched his heart's desire, his mission impossible, walk further and further away without so much as a backward glance.

Why do I like that cat so much, he questioned in his mind, when she treats me like ... like ... well, like something the cat's brought in?

He was suddenly aware of a pair of eyes studying him closely. For a split second he thought it was Tom but instantly recognised that it wasn't. A tabby he didn't know was watching him from across the road. The two cats stayed still, save for their tails that gently swished from side to side, and just stared at each other.

Mmmm ... he thought, I wonder if that's Figaro?

So he crossed over, in a kind of long sweep, almost as if he wasn't trying to alarm the other cat, and sidled up to him.

"Hello," said Alfie, tentatively, "are you Figaro?"

"Who wants to know?" came the curt response.

"My name's Alfie. Just wondered if you were Figaro."

"What if I am?"

"Just be very pleased to meet you, that's all."

"What d'you know about Figaro? Who's been talking?"

"Look, I'm sorry, no offence, just hoped to meet Figaro, nothing sinister, that's all."

"Well, just keep on looking, pussy-cat."

And the tabby rose and turned and zipped away, taking Alfie by surprise and leaving him in his wake. Alfie was no sprinter and he knew it was no good following. He remembered Patches and his words of wisdom regarding Figaro and thought he probably understood though without realising why.

Best to leave him alone. Oh well, Alfie thought very resignedly, let's go home and grab some food, nothing else is happening out here at the mo.

But it wasn't destined to be Alfie's only meeting with Figaro.

***

In due course Tom, Alfie and Hartley met up as usual under the back of Mr Simpson's car. There wasn't much to say, so there was a fair amount of paw licking and general cleaning in between periods of total rest and shut-eye. Occasionally a car would drive past or a human being or two would walk by and every now and then a pedestrian would stop to say 'ah' and such like whilst admiring the threesome. A young mother went past with her little toddler, a small girl, in tow and the toddler was so excited about the three that she just stood and waved with all her might and tried, with limited success, to say words like 'puss-puss' and 'hello' but had more success with 'goooo' and 'yehehehehe'.

It was left to mum to apply the coup-de-grace.

"Oh, Olivia, look at that lovely coloured cat, all those different colours, can you see her, Olivia, isn't she a pretty, pretty cat." Hartley sniggered under his breath. Tom rolled his eyes. Alfie was hurt.

"*She*" he muttered contemptuously, "*she* is a **he**. Huh!" With that he rolled onto his side, closed his eyes and pretended to be asleep.

Olivia meanwhile gurgled and clapped and laughed and leapt around with joy, and tried one more 'goooooo', before her mum led her gently away, still saying that the many coloured cat was so gorgeous, wasn't she?

"Wonder what it is with Figaro?" enquired Hartley, tactfully changing the subject as the mum and daughter disappeared down the road.

"Well," ventured Tom, "if he belongs to the intruder he's obviously learned some mean habits and probably treats everyone the way his service provider does, you know, rudely and suspiciously."

"Yes," added Alfie, "but we must remember what Patches said, about him possibly being a rescue cat and having had a dreadful kittenhood."

"No excuse for rudeness," Hartley intervened.

There was silence and more licking and cleaning, followed by more yawning and stretching.

"Perhaps the fox'll get him and we'll be left alone."

Tom and Alfie opened their eyes and stared at Hartley.

"Listen Hartley," Tom admonished, "we never talk like that about any cat. What a nasty thing to say. And besides, if he eats Figaro he'll definitely get a taste for cat."

"Maybe not," suggested an unfeeling Hartley, "might give him indigestion and then he'd think twice about touching cat again!"

"Too much to hope," commented Alfie who, after all, had been on the fox's menu quite recently.

Then they heard Mr Simpson coming down to his car. He was going out. Driving. How very inconvenient and thoughtless! Time for the intrepid trio to move on, and it was now Tom who suggested seeing if Auntie Joyce was back home. Hartley declined involvement and said he was heading for home and a few of the delicious biscuits Colleen always left out for him.

So Tom and Alfie set sail for Auntie Joyce.

***

Joyce Warburton was just back from Tesco and unloading her purchases. This is when I miss George, she thought, these bags are so heavy and he used to carry them in as if they weighed nothing at all! Her memory took her back all those years to her wedding and the first night they shared in their new home. They hadn't been able to afford a honeymoon and spent their first week as Mr and Mrs Warburton in the suburban semi they were buying.

George, ever the romantic, had followed tradition and carried her over the threshold amidst much laughter and humour. He simply swept her up into his arms as if she was as light as a feather!

She brought her shopping bags into the kitchen but instead of unpacking them at once made her way to the lounge. There was something she wanted to see. On the mantelpiece was their wedding day photo. My, what a gorgeous man he was, what a catch! Strong but a very gentle giant. He always treated her with kindness, respect and tenderness. Nothing was ever too much trouble and they doted on each other.

Joyce was almost embarrassed as a tear escaped and slipped down her cheek.

"Now, now, girl," she quietly admonished herself, "George wouldn't want you to cry, least of all over him." Pulling herself together, admittedly with some effort, she went back to unpacking her bags and then realised she'd left the front door open.

Reaching the front door she was conscious of two cats sitting on the drive watching her. One a tabby, one all different colours just like the one she'd seen recently.

"Wonder if she's a spare widow," whispered Alfie.

"Mmmm .... we need to get her to talk to us, just like Mr Simpson did to me when he opened up about the robbery. Let's go for the same tactics. We'll make a fuss of her if she'll let us."

"My, my, two lovely little cats, there's a nice puss-puss, there's a nice puss-puss, would you like Auntie Joyce to give you a cuddle?" Alfie winced. Goo-goo-goo, he thought to himself, drives me up the wall, I don't know!

Tom advanced and allowed Joyce to rub his throat and remembered to close his eyes and purr just like humans seem to like. It did the trick. She was all over him. Alfie winced some more. So much goo-goo-goo. But, he supposed, he'd have to make the sacrifice and do his bit, so he ambled up and let Joyce rub his neck and then turned over so she could rub his tum.

"There's a beautiful cat, *there's* a beautiful cat," she cooed, "Do you like *this*, do you *like* this, *do* you like this? Oh my word, you *love* this don't you pussy, don't you just love it." Alfie tried to pretend it was Carla rubbing his tum but it did no good. Carla wouldn't be wrapping it all up in goo-goo-goo for one thing! But he put up with it for Mr Simpson's sake.

Auntie Joyce got so carried away with Alfie, who was making a much better fist of enjoying it, that she left Tom alone for a moment. He sat on the step, tried to look hurt and failed. He was loving every moment of seeing Alfie idolised and humiliated all at the same time. A good actor!

But for all their efforts, all their over-acting, they weren't invited inside and were (politely) left on the doorstep when Auntie Joyce had decided to move. Yes, there was the frozen food to put away she suddenly realised, and she gently closed the door having wished her new feline friends farewell.

They looked at each other. Alfie sneered. He'd put up with all that goo-goo-goo for nothing. But Tom knew that it wasn't going to happen all at once and they'd have to work on Auntie Joyce.

Gradually another boiling hot summer's day wreaked havoc on those who didn't like heat and oodles of pleasure on those that loved the sun. Flowers held their heads up to the warmth of the sun's rays and other flowers cringed and withdrew, it was all too much for them.

Scantily clad humans basked in the sunshine. Others, dressed for work, sweltered and in some cases cursed. People digging holes in the road mopped sweat from their brows, an elderly couple sat on a seat under a tree in the shade and expressed their happiness at finding somewhere cool. Two youngsters joyously splashed around in the paddling pool in their garden, a bus driver stuck in traffic silently swore an oath, a Personal Assistant was grateful for the air conditioning in her boss's office, a road sweeper found a shady spot and paused for a cigarette, and three ladies in sun hats strolled along the prom making the most of the light sea breeze.

Too hot for cats.

Hartley knew of a quiet, shaded spot in the churchyard and had settled down there, revelling in spells of sleep, spells of doing nothing at all, spells of personal cleaning, spells of dozing and spells of resting. It's a hard life, he concluded!

Tom and Alfie went their separate ways, both hell bent on food, both looking forward to a period of rest away from the sun. Once they had eaten.

And Auntie Joyce, having put her shopping away, made herself a jacket potato and some salad for her lunch. She paused once more to think about dear George and then moved her thoughts along. Would love to cook for someone again, she felt, it's really quite uninteresting preparing food for one, boring really, and it's much nicer two people eating together.

She sighed. She sighed in George's memory as he had loved her cooking and then some. She sighed because she wished to cook for another once more. Be quite pleasant, she thought, to have someone to snuggle up to on the settee again!

The day tried its best for everyone. Some loved it, some loathed it. The long summer evenings were paradise for some, near torture for others. The cats weren't the only ones to feel relieved when the heat subsided, the sun set, and the first shreds of darkness of a moonless night started to fall upon Minster and the isle of Sheppey.

Relief for some cats, but not all. Disaster was assembling an unpleasant event ready to be visited on two of Minster's feline population. Neither cat knew yet the role they were going to be involuntarily asked to play. But destiny was calling as evening became night and then night became the wee small hours.

And it was in the wee small hours disaster struck.

Chapter Six

Carla passed by on the other side of the road deliberately ignoring Alfie who was concentrating on his vision of loveliness and desire. He didn't even see the dark presence moving quietly behind her in the night time blackness.

Suddenly there was a squeal and Alfie spun round in time to see the fox grab hold of Carla. Without a moment's hesitation, and with no thought for his own safety, he was across the road and up on the fox's back, clawing and spitting, but the fox shrugged him off. He had his prey and it was time to go and enjoy it.

What changed his mind was seeing Alfie sprawling on the pavement for he recognised the cat from their earlier encounter and in that second decided on a change of menu. Carla was released and Alfie seized.

"Run, Carla, run," squealed Alfie, knowing he was about to lay down his life for the girl of his dreams. And at least he had the satisfaction of seeing her dash away to safety. The fox turned for an instant to see Carla go and Alfie snatched his opportunity and managed to free himself. He was off but the fox was on his tail.

In his terror and fear Alfie could feel the fox almost breathing down his neck and knew the beast was inches rather than feet behind him. He was so gripped with fright that he never thought to twist and turn or try and leap a wall or fence. He simply sped on with all the pace he could muster.

But he was no Hartley. And he knew the end was nigh. In his panic he hoped it would be swift and painless and knew it would be neither. He was so panic struck that he didn't recognise the Minster Road right ahead and he gave no thought to the possibility of traffic, even at that hour, on the main road.

He was across the pavement in a flash, the fox right behind, ready for the kill, and didn't see the huge, heavy tipper lorry bearing down on him. The driver braked instinctively as the cat shot in front of him, and his quick reactions saved Alfie's life, for he missed being hit by the lorry by no more than a couple of inches.

For the fox so close behind there was no escape.

Alfie realised what had happened and paused to see that he was no longer being chased and in his relief crept into a garden and found some bushes to lie down under. He collapsed in a heap, exhausted, shaken, utterly spent, his legs like jelly. He was panting and wheezing and gasping but he was safe. They all were now.

As the need for sleep enveloped him he was suddenly aware that another cat was standing over him. A tabby. Was it Tom? Please let it be Tom. But no, he soon realised it was Figaro, and it was Figaro who spoke.

"Sleep, brave cat, sleep. I will watch over you. The fox will harm nobody now." And he settled down to sit close by Alfie. "You have saved us all from the fox."

"Carla?" asked Alfie anxiously, "is Carla okay?"

"If you mean the tortoiseshell, she is fine. She saw what happened and knows what a courageous cat you are. I asked and she said she was alright and then told me to clear off!"

"That's Carla," responded Alfie.

"Now Alfie, that is your name isn't it, you must sleep after your ordeal. I will not move till you wake, I promise."

Alfie stretched and feeling much better already, and far too tired to talk more, even though he wanted to, his eyes closed and sleep followed at once.

***

Alfie opened an eye and then let the other follow suit. There was a watery blue sky he could see through the leaves and he guessed it was well after dawn. And sitting looking right at him was Figaro and immediately all the memories of the fearsome night before flooded Alfie's mind.

He sat up a little and, quite naturally for a cat, started licking his paws and then other parts of his anatomy in a clean up campaign. Figaro didn't move, his eyes watching Alfie's cleaning programme.

"Are you hungry?" asked the tabby. "I could catch you a mouse for breakfast," he suggested. Alfie sat right up and politely declined the offer. He was going to be quite rude about the suggestion as he dined solely on the tasty meals Kate and Hugh dished up, and had no wish to try what he termed 'junk food'. Then he remembered what Patches had said and elected to give no offence.

"That's very kind of you, Figaro, but no, I'm not hungry at the mo."

"If you're okay then, Alfie, I'll be on my way."

"No, wait please, Figaro. Don't go. I'd like to talk to you, get to know you. Please don't go."

The two cats adjusted their positions without taking their eyes off each other. When both seemed quite comfortable Alfie spoke.

"Please tell me about Figaro."

"What's to tell?"

"A whole story, I should think, and I'd like to know." Figaro sniffed the air, rolled his eyes and turned his head away in answer to Alfie's observation.

"Nothing to tell. There's no story. And I'll be off now. Bye Alfie."

Alfie sprang up.

"Look, Figaro, please don't go. You said I was a brave cat. Well, I'm nothing of the sort. You said I've saved everyone from the fox. You have kindly watched over me, and I'm grateful, but I would like your company some more, and maybe I deserve that after all that was achieved last night. Please favour me with your company and tell me about Figaro."

"Nothing. It's all boring. You don't want to know, you don't *need* to know." And he laid down in a ball and watched Alfie from behind his front paws.

"You're very wrong, Figaro. So why don't you tell me your story?"

Figaro stretched out, yawned, and came to a decision.

"Okay, I'll tell you, for what it's worth."

And this is the story Figaro told, and in his own words:

"I don't like humans, cats or dogs. Cats are bad to me. One told me she wished I'd never been born. Cats I grew up with hissed at me, spat at me, pushed me around and stole my food.

"I don't know where I come from but I think it was a rubbish bin. I was told I was one of a litter so I guess I was taken out of a litter bin. Some of the humans I lived with thought I was a football. Forever getting kicked, I was. Sometimes the man would call me over and offer me a treat in his hand. I soon learned. It was a ruse to get me close enough to kick.

"The woman would pick me up by the scruff of the neck and chuck me out the back door. It's a cat's life being a cat, ain't it Alfie? They had a dog and that attacked me just for being there. Left the other cats alone, picked on me.

"Then one day I'm shoved in a car and taken for a 'ride in the country' so they told me. I settle down but after we've gone so far the car stops, the door opens and I'm thrown out and they drive off. No idea where I was. But I was hungry, tired, and afraid. The night came and I was very alone and really frightened but I found this building and was able to get inside and curl up for a sleep. But at first the sounds of the night made it all worse for me. I'd never heard such noises.

"In the morning I set off hoping to find the place where I lived but everywhere looked so strange. I felt so lonely I even missed being kicked! What happened next is all rather hazy but some humans I didn't know found me, fed me and made feel wanted, they were so kind. Didn't know humans were ever kind to cats.

"Anyway, I finished up in this place with other cats. Some didn't like me but one or two spoke to me, just like you've done, Alfie. So I started wondering if all cats were the same and that maybe some were different, y'know, really nice. Like you Alfie, I suppose.

"I heard them say that if I didn't find a home soon I'd be put down, so I reckoned that meant I'd have to live downstairs or something. And right out of the blue Brian and Melody appeared and adopted me, whatever that means. So here I am. They've treated me fine but I still recoil if they come near me. I expect to be kicked but they've never done that, never threatened it. Are some humans okay, Alfie?" Alfie nodded, utterly overwhelmed by what he was hearing.

"They feed me lovely grub. No other cats to steal it. They make me feel happy, but I'm still suspicious, still nervous.

"You're the only local cat I've met who has been nice to me, Alfie. Do you have any friends I could have too, or will they all shun me like the tortoiseshell did?"

Alfie felt the tears well up in his eyes. Were there really people out there who treated cats like that? How awful.

"Carla is like that with everyone, Figaro, but she doesn't mean any harm. And I'm sure my friends would love to be your friends too. Tom's a tabby and he's really great. Hartley's a marmalade and he knows the area inside out so we call him Catnav. Then there's Angus. He's got a very thick coat and he looks a bit stern but he's alright really. I'll introduce you and, don't worry, none of them would steal your food."

Alfie paused and found himself considering another point.

"Figaro, tell me about Brian."

"Brian? Why do you ask?"

"Just wondered. What he does for a living, what sort of service provider he is, that sort of thing."

Figaro looked away, licked a paw, then faced Alfie.

"He's okay. Doesn't kick me. Melody is wonderful, always very kind, gives me loads of food, and it's the best food I've ever had."

"Yes, but Brian?"

"Why the interest Alfie?"

Alfie sensed Figaro was starting to bristle and was clearly suspicious of his questions so he said it wasn't important and changed the subject, falling back on the old chestnut of discussing the weather.

Later the two cats went their separate ways in order to return home for food, but they arranged to meet again so that Figaro could be introduced to his new mates.

***

Tom was curious about why Figaro seemed unwilling to talk about Brian and was beginning to think that the cat knew something of his service provider's nocturnal career in crime. He puzzled on the matter for some time hoping to find some excuse for the cat's behaviour but found none.

If he was saddened to hear Figaro's story poor Hartley was quite overcome and moved to tears.

But as time went by and Figaro didn't appear all three cats grew suspicious. Finally Tom voiced an opinion.

"Wonder if he's telling us the truth about his kittenhood, y'know, trying to win our sympathy. Perhaps he's always lived with Brian and Melody and maybe he's not a very nice cat."

"I'll pop over his place," volunteered Hartley, "see if there's anything to see. I can be there and back in a few minutes."

"Okay," agreed Tom, "but mind the Minster Road. Remember what nearly happened to Alfie and *did* happen to the fox." And Hartley was gone. Sure enough, he returned just minutes later and said there was no sign of Figaro or, for that matter, Brian or Melody.

"Carla's approaching," advised Tom, exercising his fabled ability to identify another cat at some distance. Alfie's ears pricked up, not so much because he could hear her coming, but at the mention of her name. He sat up and automatically licked his paws which he then used to clean his face. Must look his best!

"Hello Alfie," she said as she came round the corner, "I wanted to thank you for saving my life. You are a wonderfully courageous cat and I'm very proud of you. If you would let me I'd love to have a snuggle."

There was never, ever going to be any question about it. A snuggle with Carla was more than a dream come true, it would be everything Alfie could want from life and would empty his entire wish list in one hit.

As the two cats snuggled up lovingly together, gazing into each other's eyes and occasionally giving each other a lick, Hartley whispered quietly to Tom.

"I think they're going to be an item now."

"What's an item, Hartley?"

"I don't rightly know, but I heard my service providers saying they were an item, so I think it's what happens when two people snuggle up together. Cha-cha says she wants us to be an item but I can't figure out how two cats can become one item."

"Don't lose any sleep over it, Catnav, what will be will be...."

***

Intermission

Tom writes:

"Well, while Hartley worried becoming an item, and Alfie and Carla were well on the way, our problems weren't getting solved.

"And I was starting to think that Figaro could be a problem we could do without.

"Had we found a replacement widow for Mr Simpson? We needed to accelerate our work in that direction. And I was fast coming to the conclusion that one of us was going to have to enter Figaro's home and conduct a search on the off-chance of finding the locket.

"But bringing Brian to justice might just be beyond us cats.

"As we head into chapter seven you will learn how we sorted these matters out. But inevitably things did not run smoothly. Oh well, such is life....."

Chapter Seven

Hartley was wide-eyed. He couldn't believe his ears.

"Um ... er ... Tom, we've nearly lost Angus and Alfie twice, how close do we need to sail to the wind?"

"What?"

"Er .. don't know what it means, heard it at home and thought it sounded good."

Tom despaired. Hartley using words and expressions he didn't understand. Route one to trouble, but he kept quiet on the subject, there being more important issues under debate right now.

"Look Hartley, I've been through the cat flap into Figaro's place and this time I'll be well prepared. I just need a reliable look-out."

"Just a thought, Tom, suppose Figaro's story's true, and he catches you how do you think that'll make him feel?"

"Chance we have to take. We must look for that locket."

"Okay, okay, okay. I'll be look-out. Wonder how Alfie is getting on round at Auntie Joyce's?"

Round at Auntie Joyce's Alfie was sitting patiently on the back lawn outside the patio doors from where he could see the lady indoors. He was hoping his presence would draw her out, and in this venture he had company he was delighted with.

In fact, he would've been quite happy if Carla had dogged (if you will forgive the expression in a cat novel) his every footstep from then until the end of time and beyond. He was basking in a warm glow that he assumed came from the sun whereas it probably emanated from his heart which was beating in overdrive.

The two cats sat side by side and eventually their patience and persistence paid off. Auntie Joyce saw them and came to the door before advancing onto the patio. Both cats allowed her to make a tremendous fuss of them and it was only a question of time before all that goo-goo-goo (as Alfie always termed it) revealed the information they sought.

"Oh my," Auntie Joyce gushed, "my dear George, God rest his soul, would've loved you two. If only he was here now, I'm sure he would make *such* a fuss of you, *yes* he would, yes he *would.*"

Frankly, Alfie had endured enough fuss to last a lifetime and was quite pleased Uncle George wasn't there to add to Auntie Joyce's efforts. Carla was well past the 'enough fuss' stage and provided their medium for escape by getting up and wandering up the lawn while Auntie Joyce was fully occupied fussing over Carla's saviour.

Unwilling to be separated from his great love Alfie sprang to his feet and set off after her.

"Come back any time. Auntie Joyce will always be pleased to see you." Yes, thought Alfie, we'll be back because Tom will have a masterplan for bringing you and Mr Simpson together! And if I'm a lucky cat it will be a masterplan for avoiding all that goo-goo-goo. By now Carla had leapt a fence so Alfie followed expecting her to be well ahead of him. She wasn't. She was waiting for him and wanted a snuggle.

He still couldn't believe all his dreams were coming true and felt sure he would wake up and find none of it had ever happened. But it was very real, and Carla was very real indeed as she snuggled herself tightly up to her hero. My, how she purred! But then so did Alfie. Very, very much.

***

Meanwhile Tom and Hartley had arrived at their destination. The car wasn't there so presumably Brian wasn't home but what of Melody and Figaro? Time for a look-see.

Both cats crept cautiously round to the rear of the property to make observations but stopped when they heard a noise from the front. Hartley slipped back and was in time to see a woman closing the front door behind her. This was presumably Melody and she was going out. Perfect. Just a worry about Figaro now.

Seconds later the cats were in the back garden and looking for any signs that Figaro was indoors or in the vicinity.

Tom listened intently. Not a sound and his keen ears would've picked up the movement of another cat without a doubt. He re-assured Hartley that if he detected Figaro's presence inside he would be straight back out, and with that (and his heart in his mouth) he nipped through the cat flap.

If he had been a human being he would've wiped the sweat from his brow it really had been that unnerving. But he was in. No sign of the cat. Tom sniffed the air and edged slowly forward across the kitchen. He was quite confident no other cat had been this way in some while so hopefully Figaro was not at home.

Hartley looked all around him, shaking with fear. He felt worse now than when he did getting the fox to chase him.

Tom moved further indoors. No sound, no cat scent, no movement. Still feeling wary, frightened and uneasy he explored the downstairs without any obvious success but of course he couldn't open cupboards and drawers. Then he sprang up the stairs and found himself in the bathroom. Dirty things everywhere, towels, underwear, socks, he'd never seen anything so untidy.

One bedroom door was shut, the other two ajar. He tried what he suspected was the main bedroom and realised untidiness was what Brian and Melody lived in. Clothes scattered hither and thither. He nimbly leapt onto the dressing table and found items of Melody's jewellery lying about but no locket. He cursed the fact he couldn't open the drawers and cursed himself for not thinking of that.

Not that he would've come up with a solution even if he had done.

But what was this? One cupboard was slightly open! He nudged the door and slipped inside. All very dark and in fairness he knew he wasn't likely to find anything there. What he did find was a pair of eyes. It startled the life out of him. They were staring at him in the darkness from behind a couple of coats.

A voice, presumably having a connection with the eyes, spoke.

"You've come for me, haven't you? I saw you from up here, knew you'd all come for me, and I thought I could hide here. You're all going to attack me, aren't you? That's what cats do. Please leave me alone. I don't want to be attacked anymore."

Tom took a step back and pushed the cupboard door open wider so that light could fall on the scene. Figaro winced, though whether from the light, or from fear, or from resignation it was impossible to say. Tom looked at him.

"Figaro, just listen to me. We are friends. I am not here to attack you. Please let me explain."

Figaro sat back on his hind legs and sank down with his head on his front paws. Tom took this to mean that he should go ahead with his explanation.

"We think Brian is not a good man. He may be kind to you, but we think he robbed an elderly man of something very precious, a gold locket containing photos of a nostalgic nature, valuable photos, Figaro. Valuable to the old man. Irreplaceable photos.

"I have come into your home thinking you weren't here, not to attack you, but to try and find that locket because it doesn't belong to Brian. You have nothing to fear. We are truly your friends as you will discover if you let us into your world and your life."

Tom made a bold decision, and one he was not authorised to make.

"If we find the locket and can return it nobody will be any the wiser, so nothing will happen to Brian. You can carry on living here with him and with Melody. But I cannot be responsible if the law catches up with him. He shouldn't be robbing people, Figaro."

Figaro tried to weigh up everything he'd been told and licked his paws a few times.

"I don't know I can believe you. Cats and humans lie to me when they want to hurt me...."

"No, Figaro," interrupted Tom, "it's not like that. I'm not lying to you. Come and meet my friends, Alfie you already know and you trust him, surely? Come and find out for yourself. We can be your friends forever and you can share so much fun with us. And I am also telling you the truth about Brian. Come and meet Angus and he will tell you the story.

"In fact, Angus owes his life to Brian, well, indirectly. So I don't suppose he'll want anything to happen to Brian. We just want to try and find that locket."

There was a pause as both cats studied each other. Figaro had learned to trust nobody. But on reflection what had he to lose? If it went well it would be wonderful. If (what was the expression Brian used? Ah yes, pear-shaped) it all went pear-shaped then he wouldn't be any worse off.

"I'm Tom, if you didn't know, and Hartley is outside. Come out and meet him."

Figaro gingerly followed his fellow tabby downstairs, through the kitchen, and out the cat flap to where Hartley greeted them in open-eyed amazement.

"Let's go and meet Angus," said Tom, "and he can tell Figaro his tale."

***

"And that's it. If Brian hadn't fallen over me and the fox I'd have been a gonner, so I actually owe him my life," Angus explained. At that point Carla and Alfie arrived with their own story to tell and Alfie rushed to greet his new friend. Carla, seeing this, and not wishing to be left out of anything Alfie was doing, followed suit and suddenly Figaro was not only the centre of attention, he was in danger of being smothered with affection.

Alfie turned to Carla and explained how, after he laid down completely exhausted following the incident with the fox, Figaro had stood guard while he slept. This made Carla even more affectionate to Figaro.

And Figaro discovered he rather liked affection. Better than being kicked, anyway.

And Figaro discovered he had some new and very genuine friends, and that was *much* better than being kicked.

In due course Tom tactfully turned the conversation back to Mr Simpson, Auntie Joyce and, of course, the missing locket. He told Figaro all about the situation and asked if he knew if Brian was involved in crime. Figaro drew breath and, after a moment's hesitation, spoke.

"Well, Melody did once call him a petty thief. But I've never known what a petty is or why he would want to steal one. I don't think he's ever brought one home. She also called him a waste of space and asked him why he didn't get a proper job. So he got a proper job and Melody was pleased especially when he promised to give up burglary.

"In a quiet moment when she was cuddling me, and Brian was at work, she told me he was cat burglar but I don't remember him stealing any cats either. Then I wondered if that meant he would steal my food given half a chance, but he never did.

"I thought he'd given up crime, but he hasn't. Melody would be so upset if she knew. And to think he's stolen that gold locket. All I can do for the moment is have a good scout round when I go home. I can seize any chance of course. If they open a drawer I can be there in a split second. More chance with them both around tonight.

"But I don't want Brian to get into trouble. Melody told me he'd been inside once, but she never said inside what. I guess it wasn't nice being inside whatever it was."

All the cats voiced their approval of Figaro's intentions and Tom said he would give some thought to keeping Brian outside rather than inside.

***

It was Figaro who came up with the idea. It seemed outrageous at first. Angus couldn't help thinking that crime was central to Figaro's world, but kept his thoughts to himself. The idea was initially shot down in flames as it did indeed involve crime. But a seed had been sown and over the next few minutes the cats found themselves discussing the possibility, and dismissing their earlier disinterest. Enthusiasm started to wash over them all.

And, of course, it was Tom who was left to organise it!

Chapter Eight

Sadly Figaro had to report back that he had found nothing so far, but that there were one or two possibilities that it hadn't yet been practical to explore. He would try again another time.

The next day was when they put Figaro's idea and Tom's resultant plan into action.

The postman was whistling cheerfully as he approached Mr Simpson's. He had something for every address and was too busy with his job to notice a positive bevy of cats assembling nearby.

As he reached Mr Simpson's Carla, Cha-cha, Angus and Bubbles went into action.

With a great deal of meow-ing and purring they put themselves in the postman's way. As hoped, he turned out to be a cat lover and bent down to apply goo-goo-goo to the cats who pretended to lap it all up. They were putty in his hands, one of which held two letters for (they assumed) Mr Simpson.

Like lightning Hartley leapt upon the scene, took the postman by surprise, snatched the letters from his grip and sped off. As if responding to the postman's cry Hartley stopped dead and looked back, both letters in his mouth. He promptly dropped the pair of them, whereupon Tom dashed past and grabbed one and was away. The poor postman didn't know which cat to follow and confusion momentarily reigned.

The postman retrieved the remaining letter as the cats scattered at speed. If he looked bemused, he might well have done. He knocked on Mr Simpson's door and explained to an equally incredulous Mr Simpson what had happened. They discussed the extraordinary scene the postman had witnessed. Neither could really work out what had occurred other than a cat had now absconded with one of the old gentleman's pieces of mail. There was simply no explanation for the astonishing event.

Neither had ever heard of such a thing. They were truly amazed and bewildered.

Out of their sight Tom passed the letter to Alfie. Now for stage two.

***

Alfie arrived in Auntie Joyce's back garden with the letter in his mouth, and he sat on the lawn where he had sat before, and from where he could see the old lady. Unwilling to be too far from his side Carla sat on the top of the fence.

It only took a couple of minutes before Auntie Joyce saw the cat and as usual set off to goo-goo-goo him. As she stepped onto the patio she saw the letter which Alfie duly dropped. The plan was going very smoothly, he felt. She picked up the letter, noted the name and address out loud, and the words were precisely what Alfie needed to hear.

Of course, she wanted to know what Alfie was doing with it and Alfie wasn't about to tell her. It was only when she said she was going to look at his collar to see if there was a contact number for him that he knew it was time to go. And he went, went like the wind, with Carla alongside.

But, thus far, the plan had worked. The one drawback was if Auntie Joyce put the letter in the postbox or simply put it through Mr Simpson's letterbox. The cats wanted her to go to his home, knock and actually speak to him. It was time for them to all hold their breaths. And wait.

***

Tom had drawn up a duty roster to keep an eye on Mr Simpson's and on Auntie Joyce's and to report any relevant action. They didn't have long to wait.

He was on duty himself when Angus reported that Auntie Joyce was on the move, and this time she made her way round to Mr Simpson's.

Tom and Angus, making good use of available cover, moved stealthily closer to the front door, hopefully keeping out of sight. Tom's heart missed a beat. She took the letter out of her handbag and rang the doorbell. Tom looked at Angus and Angus looked at Tom. Paws crossed, thought Angus, paws crossed.

The door opened and Auntie Joyce spoke first.

"Oh good afternoon, are you by any chance Mr Simpson?"

"Yes, I am,"

"Well, this is going to sound so strange," and she gave a little girlish giggle, "but, you probably won't believe this, but a cat appeared in my garden with this letter in its mouth and I think it's addressed to you."

"Well, goodness gracious me," replied an incredulous Albert Simpson, "well I never, well I never. But I have to tell you something stranger still, Mrs .... er .... Mrs...."

"Mrs Warburton, I'm Joyce Warburton," she offered swiftly.

Auntie Joyce Warburton. Auntie Joyce Warburton, reflected Tom. That's a nice name, Warburton. At least you can tell she must be well bred......

Within moments Auntie Joyce had been invited inside to hear the extraordinary story of the 'stolen' letter, and the cats held their breath.

Was this the start of something, the very thing the cats had set out to achieve? Well, it was up to the humans now, the cats had done all they could. Mr Simpson and Mrs Warburton were together and talking.

***

They were not the only couple talking.

Melody was having an attack of what Brian might have called the screaming abdabs. And Brian was the cause.

She couldn't believe it. He was showing her the locket and she was having kittens.

"You've bin thievin' again, you fool, you idiot. My God, you'll be going inside again. Why did I have to finish up with you? I should've listened to mum, she knew, she knew what a useless, clueless bloke you are. Gawd strewth! Stop pinching things or – we – are - *finished, do – you – un - der – stand?*"

And with that she tore at her hair and let out a suppressed scream. Figaro has hiding under the table, shaking. Brian had been pleased with himself and wanted to show off his ill-gotten gains. Bad mistake.

Brian now understood. Melody was giving him his last chance and he knew it. Old habits were finding it hard to die, but he really did have to crack it this time. He loved his Melody and he'd let her down so often, and he realised he had to reform and pronto. He had a good job and it paid quite well, they had a decent home, they got on well and enjoyed their time together.

No, he didn't need to steal again, ever. But what about the locket?

"Um ... Mel .. what can I do about the locket?"

"Oh, just leave it be, I'll think of something. Please, please, promise me that this time it's for good. Go straight or you'll be going straight out the door. I mean it Bri."

She meant it and he knew it. Now or never.

"Mel, this time, this time I'll do it. Promise."

And she came to his side, delivered a mighty slap round his face and then hugged and hugged him and both wept tears. Figaro was totally baffled. Why do humans have to hit each other and kick cats, he queried in his mind. Strange world.

"Right, this is what we'll do. Throw that thing in the bin. It'll go out in the wheelie and be gone forever. Never, ever bring anything stolen into this house again." Brian nodded furiously, rubbed his sore cheek, and took the locket to the kitchen. Figaro followed at what he hoped was a safe distance.

The locket went in the kitchen bin above the sink. Brian went back to the lounge to seek even more forgiveness from Melody as she seemed to be in a very forgiving mood, all things considered. Figaro sprang up onto the draining board full of excitement only to have his hopes dashed when he saw the locket had sunk down in the bin. Past the teabags. Past the used tissues. Past the chocolate wrappers. The chain was barely visible.

But he knew this was his big moment, his chance to prove himself worthy of his new friends. He knew he mustn't muck up.

Yet how to get that locket out of the bin without the bin falling over as it surely would when he reached over it, and he found himself wishing Tom was there as he now knew Tom had an answer for most things.

What would Tom do, he asked himself? If he knocked the bin over the clatter would bring one or both service providers to the kitchen and the game would be up. It was *his* moment, make or break, and he became conscious of the fact he was hot and shaking, as nervous as can be.

***

Auntie Joyce Warburton had long departed Albert Simpson's and she had spent quite some time inside too, so the cats, albeit on tenterhooks, were cautiously hopeful. They had heard Mr Simpson say 'see you tomorrow, then, Joyce' as they said their goodbyes on the doorstep. He'd offered to run her home but she'd declined, but at least they were on first name terms and were seeing each other again.

So Tom, Angus, Alfie and, yes, Carla had settled down together under the gentleman's car. Carla was never far from Alfie and Alfie was positively delighted with the arrangement.

"Here comes Figaro," announced Tom, yet again demonstrating his propensity for recognising an approaching cat before it came into view. They all looked up as the tabby made its leisurely way across the road, but mainly to see that Tom had got it right yet again.

Then they all sat up.

Then they all got up, for Figaro had something shiny in his mouth and they quickly realised it was the missing locket. And balanced on his head was a used teabag.

He was welcomed into the group like a long lost friend and Carla helped remove the teabag that had become stuck to his hairs as he related his yarn.

He'd overcome his problem by stretching right up on his back legs and then, rather like an inverted U-bend, had leaned clean over the top of the bin, grabbed the chain, become attached to the teabag in the process, and been able to remove himself and the locket without knocking the bin over.

Phew!

Now what? How to return it to Mr Simpson?

Tom (naturally) came up with the answer.

The five cats went up to the front door and Figaro laid the locket on the step. Then they set about a rendition of the cats chorus which certainly did the trick. Mr Simpson was obviously unhappy when he opened his door to find five assorted cats me-owing furiously on his drive.

But his annoyance vanished when he looked down and saw the locket. He couldn't quite take it all in and he certainly couldn't understand. He gently reached down and retrieved the locket, his hands trembling as much as his lips were doing. He held the locket for some while, just staring at it and slowly shaking his head as his eyes moistened, before he clasped his fingers around it and allowed the soft tears to roll down his cheeks.

However, there was one more thing to do and sadly it was the one thing the cats didn't have the wherewithal and ability to check: were the photos still inside?

Gingerly Mr Simpson freed the clasp (no cat could've done it), looked down and his tears became a torrent as his shoulders heaved and he uttered the words 'Oh Emily, my darling Emily'. For a moment the cats were transfixed, all too afraid the photos had been removed, so you could imagine their relief when he turned the locket round to show them the two pictures intact.

"I don't know what you cats had to do with this," he wept, "probably nothing. But maybe everything. I don't know. It's just that ... well ... my instinct is telling me you all had something to do with this. Don't ask me why I think that. Now, I don't suppose any of you would like a cuddle from a very grateful old man?" He knelt down in the doorway and much to his surprise was overwhelmed by five very friendly, very beautiful, lovely cats of all colours, every one of them very much wanting a cuddle with an equally happy old gentleman.

Epilogue

Tom writes:

"What an adventure! Well, time has passed by and I can report on developments.

"Mr Simpson and Mrs Warburton have become very close friends and time alone will tell. We cats often pop by both properties and we're always made to feel most welcome. They are an elderly couple and will not be rushing into anything which is very wise, but they seem to be a very happy together and we dream on.

"The good news is that Hartley and Cha-cha are proud parents to a lovely litter of six marmalade kittens. No doubt each kitten will have its own name, but we cats had great fun (bearing in mind the names of the parents) coming up with nicknames for the kittens!

"In the end we settled on Robertson, Polka, Samba, Apricot, Tiptree and Can-can. Perhaps you can think of some yourself.

"Immediately after our adventure drew to a close we all went down to see Patches to tell him our story. He listened very patiently, even when we all tried to speak at once, smiled in a knowing sort of way, and said he was very pleased with us and the way things had turned out.

"He also welcomed Figaro to the fold. Since then Figaro has advised us that Brian does indeed seem to be going straight and his relationship with Melody is even better and far more loving than it hitherto appeared. Consequently their cat is receiving greater loving attention so everyone is happy.

"That doesn't alter the fact that Brian was a thief. By that curious turn of fate that night Brian, doing a spot of burglary, indirectly saved Angus's life by falling over him and the fox. Angus said he owed his life to Brian and, since the locket had been returned, was anxious not to pursue the criminal, especially as he had appeared to reform.

"Rightly or wrongly we all accepted that (even Patches had nodded sagely) so we let the matter rest. Not that we cats could've done anything about it anyway. So it all worked out for the best.

"Life has been somewhat quieter since those sweltering hot days of that summer. Alfie spends most of his time in a daze, swamped by his feelings for Carla and overcome that his hopeless yet enchanting dream has come true. Real life's not like that, surely? The pair of them are rarely apart. Carla is still snooty (but not with Alfie) and holds her nose in the air, so we've nicknamed them the Duke and Duchess of Catford!

"Me? Well, I still wander about at my leisure, meet up with the gang (Patches calls us the Minster Moggies!) and share a natter. Thankfully we live in relative peace once more, that is, until the next adventure. If anything happens I will try and let you know, but don't hold your breath, we cats like it like this!"

Tom Vanishes

The sequel to this book is now available on Kindle from Amazon, search for Tom Vanishes to read the next instalment from Tom.

The inspiration for Tom is a real life cat of the same name, but who lives in another part of Kent. Shortly after Tom Investigates was published real life Tom left home and disappeared without trace.

Months went by, well, nine of them to be precise. And then, as if by magic, he turned up on the doorstep!

About the author

After a widely varied career, and now being retired, it has come to this: writing for fun!

My first work was *"Deadened Pain"* – a parody of the crime novel genre, and in fact there are two as yet unpublished sequels. Watch this space!

I'm a recent convert to crime novels and have read dozens in the last few years. So my work parodies the style in a satirical way, mixing humour, drama, suspense, terror, romance and a complexity of plot in what I hope is a thoroughly enjoyable read.

There are serious messages too, especially relating to illegal drugs and prejudices. In the sequels I include concern over corruption, modern slavery and mental illness in the same way.

I've spent most of my working life in travel, even running my own tour firm for a while, but have since driven lorries and a bus, worked for local councils, latterly in refuse and recycling, and had a brief spell as a Community Rail Partnership Officer on the Sheerness branch in Kent.

Finally, before retiring, a glorious three years in customer service at a branch of McDonalds where I won an employee of the month award! In fact most of my career has been in customer service of one sort or another, and it may be that some of the people I've met and worked with over the years have inspired some of the characters I've created.

A proud Londoner by birth I have come to love Essex and Kent and have settled in the latter these last 40-odd years, the isle of Sheppey being my current home.

So unsurprisingly my second book is entitled *"Sheppey Short Stories – Tall Tales from North Kent"*. It's a collection of completely varied stories featuring humour, satire, romance and sadness, with relationships being the central theme.

The *Tom* stories happened by chance for I've never had a cat! And there's a sequel to *"Tom Investigates"* called *"Tom Vanishes"*.

As yet unpublished is a sort of romantic story called "*After Hugh*". And my first serious work, a novel based in the late 18th century east Kent called "*Kindale*" – a story of menace, intrigue, treachery, espionage and crime against a backdrop of the fear of invasion at a time when smuggling was rife.

Printed in Great Britain
by Amazon

22038707R00036